ONE BEAR EXTRAORDINAIRE

EXTRAORDINAIRE

JAYME McGOWAN

Abrams Books for Young Readers
New York

A NOTE ABOUT THE ART

Jayme McGowan creates her art by a process of three-dimensional illustration. First, she sketches a pencil outline on new, recycled, or repurposed paper, and then she adds details and shades of color with ink, colored pencil, and watercolor paint. She cuts out each piece of paper by hand with a craft knife or scissors and carefully assembles the pieces using tweezers and glue in order to build her characters, layer by layer. She then stages miniature scenes in a paper theater approximately the size of this book, using wire, string, toothpicks, and clothespins to hold everything in place. When the scene is complete, she takes dozens of photographs, with a variety of camera settings, lenses, and light.

Library of Congress Cataloging-in-Publication Data

McGowan, Jayme, author, illustrator.
One bear extraordinaire / by Jayme McGowan.
pages cm
Summary: Every morning Bear wakes up with a song in his head, but one day he realizes the song needs something more and sets out to find what is missing, gathering a band of animal musicians along the way.
ISBN 978-1-4197-1654-6
[1. Music—Fiction. 2. Bands (Music)—Fiction. 3. Animals—Fiction.] I. Title.
PZ7.1.M436One 2015
[E]—dc23
2014041316

Text and illustrations copyright © 2015 Jayme McGowan
Book design by Alyssa Nassner

Printed and bound in China
10 9 8 7 6 5 4 3 2 1

Abrams Books for Young Readers are available at special discounts when purchased in quantity for premiums and promotions as well as fundraising or educational use. Special editions can also be created to specification. For details, contact specialsales@abramsbooks.com or the address below.

THE ART OF BOOKS SINCE 1949
115 West 18th Street
New York, NY 10011
www.abramsbooks.com

FOR JOHN

BEAR woke up one morning with a song in his head. But, of course, Bear *always* woke up with a song in his head.

Bear was a rambling musician. An entertainer. A legend.
One bear extraordinaire.

He was known across the wilderness for
his nimble paws, honey harmonies, and twinkle-toed grace.

But today, as Bear tried to play this *particular*
song, it didn't make the forest dance
the way he expected it to.

His song DROOPED...

WILTED in midair...

and CRASHED to the ground.

"Something is missing," he thought.
"I don't know what it is."

"But I'm going to find it."

Bear looked high.

Bear looked low.

He whistled for his song.
He called out.

And a banjo answered!

"Bear, where are you headed?" asked Fox.

"Just going where the music takes me," Bear replied.

"There's something I'm trying to find."

"May I come along?" asked Fox.
Bear looked at the road ahead,
and then he looked at Fox.
"Sure, why not?" he answered.

So they walked and they wandered, on and on, down past
the thicket, where they heard an accordion through the ferns.

"Where are you going?" asked Raccoon.
"Wherever the tune leads us," Bear replied.

"May I join you?" asked Raccoon.
Bear nodded.

And so they trekked and they tramped, on and on,
into the valley, where they heard a fiddle on the wind.

"Where are you off to?" asked Rabbit.

Bear gestured down the trail. "This way, I think."

"Mind if I tag along?" asked Rabbit.

"Follow us," Bear answered.

They footslogged and frolicked, on and on, through
the woods, where they heard a rustling from behind.

"HEY!" Wolf Pup cleared his throat. "What about me, Bear? I want to be a musician! What can *I* play?"

"Hmm. I don't know if we need another instrument," said Bear, "but I suppose everyone's got *something* to add."

"Here you go, Pup.
Try one of these."

But Wolf Pup DRUMMED to a different beat.

He SHOOK a strange, strange song.

He CHEWED a mysterious melody only he could hear.

He STRUMMED an unusual sound.

"Well, all that's left now is the kazoo," said Bear.
"It might be just the thing for you, little tyke. *Anyone* can play it."

The travelers reached a clearing on the mountain just as the sun was setting.
Bear built a campfire while the others tuned their instruments.

As the moon came out, Bear picked his guitar. Fox plucked his banjo.
Raccoon squeezed his accordion. Rabbit bowed his fiddle.

The campfire popped and crackled.

"That sounds pretty good," Bear said to himself,
"but *something* is still missing."

ALL OF A SUDDEN...

Out came a sound so wild and wondrous
the entire forest jumped up to listen.

"THAT'S IT! That's what
this song needed all along!"

"We've got ourselves a singer!" Bear said.